IMPOSSIBLE
CONVERSATIONS

IMPOSSIBLE
CONVERSATIONS

*Imaginary Interviews
with World-Famous Artists*

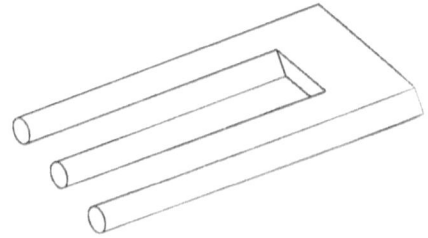

Carla M. Wilson

BLACK SCAT BOOKS
2015

Impossible Conversations
by Carla M. Wilson

ISBN-13: 978-0-692-44070-4

Cover art & book design by Norman Conquest

ACKNOWLEDGEMENTS:

Hal Jaffe – Thanks for your mentorship, and for teaching me how to begin. Thanks also for your guidance on the book's concept, and for your edits and advice, especially on Warhol, Ono, Vincent & Gauguin.

Eckhard Gerdes – Huge thanks for your friendship, for reviewing and commenting on the manuscript, and for inviting me to read, and reading excerpts from the book with me at the 2015 &Now Conference in Valencia, CA.

Katie Farris – Thanks for reviewing and commenting on some of the earliest drafts of the book, and for your invaluable edits on Hitchcock.

Ryan Forsythe – Thank you for your generosity and support; and for reviewing and commenting on the manuscript.

Derek Pell – Infinite thanks! Without your enthusiasm, patience, friendship and support, this project would never have been possible.

Norman Conquest – Thanks for taking a chance on me and my writing, for your editorial expertise, and for helping me stay curious, mischievous and always inspired.

Mother, Dad, and Alfred Wilson – Thanks for being my dear family: your loving energy and support have kept me going.

Black Scat Books
Sublime Art & Literature
BlackScatBooks.com

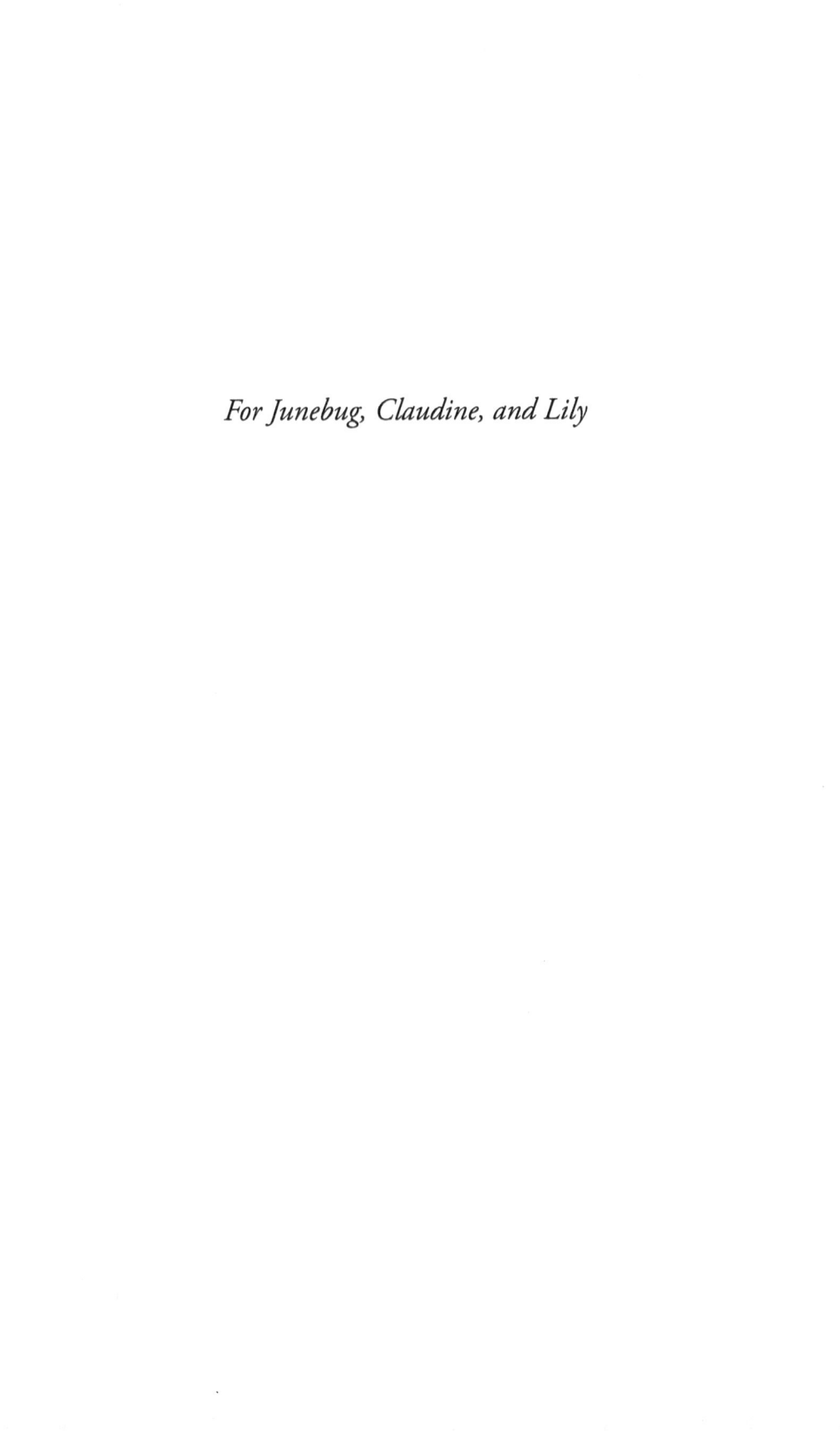

For Junebug, Claudine, and Lily

TABLE OF CONTENTS

Introduction

I can hardly believe over three years have passed since I first began writing *Impossible Conversations*. In fact, it's hard to believe I've finished an entire volume of imaginary interviews. From the book's inception, I had a vague sense of the artists I wanted to interview, but I wasn't sure how they would be linked, whether I wanted to focus on cultural commentary or rely on the artists themselves to speak out. I never thought I would become as involved in the research as extensively as I did. I had intended to base the interviews on knowledge acquired from my graduate studies in art history, relying mainly on my imagination because after all, I was writing fiction!

I was in the second year of my M.F.A. program and we were exploring flash fiction. While reading Yoko Ono's *Grapefruit* I was excited to discover that I could create a kind of "conceptual writing" that combined references to both the artist's conceptual sensibilities and my own expression within one piece of short fiction.

I also found inspiration while viewing a series of French New Wave and Italian Neorealist films, analyzing them in terms of narrative content, form, and style. The list was extensive, and included directors such as Godard, Truffaut, Vittorio De Sica, Marguerite Duras and Claire Denis, among many others. I began thinking of writing a series of homages to artists, writers and filmmakers, and *Impossible Conversations* was conceived.

By the end of my MFA program I had completed *Yoko Ono*, *Warhol*, and *Hitch* and was determined to keep working after graduation. During the summer of 2013 research became a priority. I began scouring used bookstores for art books and serendipitously found titles on the very artists I wanted to research. I also found connections with regard to birth and death dates of some of the artists. For example, while Van Gogh and Gauguin were living in the Yellow House at Arles, Man Ray, Duchamp and Georgia O'Keeffe were being born in various parts of the world, and there were other coincidences as well. None of this connectivity was planned, nor had I intended to only interview deceased artists (Yoko Ono excluded). One artist seemed to inspire the next, until I began to realize there was a pattern as I progressed. That pattern had more to do with my own quirky affinities and influences than with choosing favorite artists.

The creative flow was interrupted in 2014 when I moved from a house to an apartment, but with encouragement from my publisher, I was re-inspired and determined to continue. I decided that, in addition to choosing artists whose personalities figure prominently and have general resonance in contemporary culture, I would also include a good mix of male and female artists, and explore personas that had been connected to Dada, Surrealism, mysticism, or spirituality. I have always been interested in the psychological aspects of dreams and the fantastic worlds of imaginary beings. I've been a lifelong fan of murder mysteries and detective stories, as well, but knew little about Agatha Christie or Hitchcock personally. I chose Dada artists to include an element of humor and the absurd. In summary, I wanted the book to include all my favorite things.

Ultimately I began to see that, for me, understanding art has a great deal to do with understanding the individual artist and his or her process in art-making. I include myself in this story. While this book begins with Yoko Ono in a demonstrably experimental form, it ends with Agatha Christie in an outwardly traditional, yet metafictional narrative. At the same time, those two artists bookend symbolically my education in reverse. I hope that in reading these imaginary dialogues you will be somewhat educated as well as entertained, and that you enjoy interacting with each of these artists as much as I did. Of course the list of potential conversations is endless, but achieving that would certainly be impossible.

–Carla M. Wilson
San Diego, California
July 2015

YOKO ONO

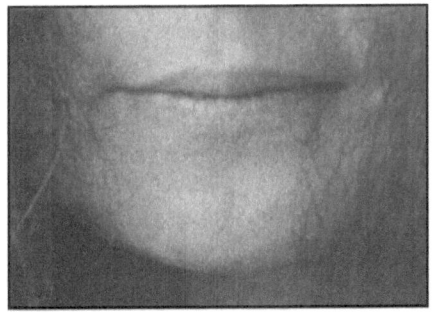

*"Count the clouds
name them."*
– Yoko Ono

Build a house
that serves only to make way for
moonlight

You wrote that in 1965 in *Grapefruit?*

Right.

One of several performance pieces from a series?

"8 Architecture Pieces dedicated to a Phantom Architect."

Conceptual art?

I call them *Events.*

Like *Happenings?*

Happenings were *Happenings.*

Happenings occurred in actual venues. Your "performances" happen in the mind.

Maybe.

If the pieces aren't performable, how do they function?

As *Events.* An Event is an Event. A Happening is a Happening. *A stein is a stone is a stone.*

I'm trying to process that.

See the spaces between. Silence. It will be what you want it to be.

Like in your *Count Piece*?

Count

count the clouds
name them

Here you require that the performance take place on the

eighth day of the series. Why?

On the ninth day there may be fewer clouds to count.

Okay.

What else?

You were part of *Fluxus*?

I performed with *Fluxus*, and then I met John.

Fluxus' aesthetic was anti-art, anti-commercialism, similar to Dada, no?

(Yoko yawns)

Fluxus paved the way for a new definition of art, no?

I'm hungry.

A minute more, please. Tell me one of your favorites.

Light Piece

Carry an empty bag
Go to the top of the hill
Pour all the light you can in it
Go home when it is dark.
Hang the bag in the middle of your
Room in place of a lightbulb.

Your pieces deal with nature and intuition. What about pain?

It exists in the world that is not a world.

Like the world of moonlit houses?

Sure. Any other questions?

What do you think of Any Warhol?

I liked him better when he was Japanese.

WARHOL

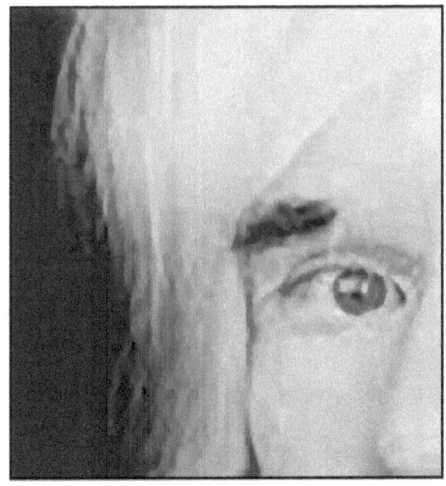

"Before I was shot, I always thought that I was more half-there than all-there —
I always suspected that I was watching TV instead of living life."
– Andy Warhol

You died in 1987. Was it you that toured San Diego in 1981?

I don't remember.

There was a rumor you were spotted at a coffee shop in La Jolla where all the artists and writers hung out. Another rumor was that it wasn't you but someone disguised as you.

The eighties were such a blur.

Was it you or not you?

Um.

Someone wearing a wig?

Um.

How would one know the real you?

I don't. . . know.

Can we talk about the shooting?

My films?

You were shot in the chest in 1968 by groupie Valerie Solanas and you barely survived.

Valerie?

You never read her script, *Up Your Ass*, or her *Scum Manifesto*?

I don't think she liked me.

She was violently abused for many years by her father, then turned to prostitution.

I guess I lost the script, or the Supes trashed it.

Supes?

They hung around The Factory. My entourage.

Edie Sedgwick, Nico, Candy Darling, Ultra Violet? Drag queen porn stars, dilettantes and socialites? They trashed Valerie's script?

[*Assistant*]: Andy gets dozens of crackpots asking him to read their work, produce films; photograph their relatives. All that shit. He's real busy.

You shot the film *San Diego Surf* in La Jolla in 1981, apparently when you weren't here.

La Jolla was so cool.

With a fake Andy with fake Andy hair in La Jolla?

I love the silver Pacific.

***San Diego Surf* is being released now, 32 years later, and is being shown at the MOMA in New York.**

Oh.

Would you tell us about it?

We were making a film about surf life. You know, the Beach Boys? We rented a huge mansion at the beach. Nobody wanted to work.

The Lotus Life, right?

What does that mean? [Looks at his assistant]

Weren't you, or whoever impersonated you, and your entourage, busted for drugs?

I think so.

So, you *were* in San Diego in 1981?

Um.

Your real name is *Andrew Varchola, right?*

[*To his assistant*]: What's my real name?

[*Assistant*]: Andy Warhol.

Your art tends to exploit American consumer culture.

What?

Your art: your mass-Factory-produced lithographs depicting pop-stars and pop-culture in all its glory—Hollywood icons, actors, musicians, famous wealthy people, controversial politicians, every day household objects like ads for soup cans and collections of shoes, the Eight Elvises—those unnaturally colored lithographs were meant to comment on the superficiality of American consumer culture, by way of theme and medium, no? Using the repetition of objects you meant to render them devoid of meaning, and the people depicted in your portraits devoid of personality, right?

Do you like them?

Well, I like some of them.

That is so groovy.

You suffered as a child from a debilitating illness, right? Stayed in bed a lot? Didn't fit in with the kids at school?

I like staying in bed all day. Watching TV.

Any comment on how that experience influenced you as an artist?

I've gotta pee.

Is it true you never use a public restroom?

I'm not sure.

Yet you photographed hundreds of young man peeing or otherwise displaying their penis.

I guess so.

Your porn star friends never did much, yet you kept them around, like a circus. Why the fascination with celebrities?

I just love beautiful people. Don't you?

Elizabeth Taylor, Marilyn Monroe, Sophia Loren, Mick Jagger, David Bowie, Jim Morrison . . . Any favorites?

Lisa Marie.

Lisa Marie Presley?

Love her.

Do you mean Lisa Marie before she was married to Michael Jackson?

What?

Before, during, or after her brief marriage to Michael Jackson?

Um, after.

Who had more marriages, Liz Taylor or Lisa Marie?

Liz. Lisa Marie was only married four times.

Weren't they close? Liz and Lisa?

That was Michael Jackson.

Now both are dead.

Dead, yes.

Which brings me back to my initial question: *Were* you in San Diego and La Jolla, or was it one of your cronies impersonating you?

Isn't La Jolla called the Jewel of the Pacific?

There are rumors you had assistants producing work instead of you, true or false?

I think you mean Picasso.

[*Assistant*]: Sometimes work bores him.

Then it's conceivable someone could have impersonated you at any time? Even now.

Um. I'm not sure.

I'm not getting any traction. Maybe I should go interview someone else.

Don't go. I hate to be alone.

Was it you, or wasn't it?

[*Assistant*]: Ask him about his films.

You and Paul Morrissey produced several underground films, including *Chelsea Girls* and *Blow Job*. You've been compared to Jean-Luc Godard.

Breathless is a good movie. I can't decide who I like better: Godard or Hitchcock.

Pick one.

Hitchcock, I guess. He had this thing for blondes.

HITCH

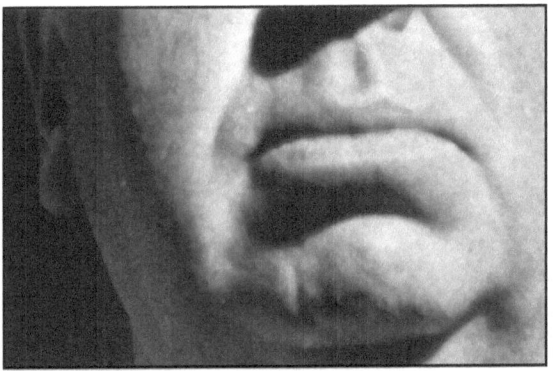

"Blondes make the best victims. They're like virgin snow that shows up the bloody footprints."
– Alfred Hitchcock

Projected against a white screen: a silhouette of a smallish head, nose, protruding round belly.

A green light blinks on:

"Good evening. Permit me to introduce myself. . ."

We're sitting at the Waldorf-Astoria Hotel bar, between takes. His lips are pursed, his voice baritone, his accent of course British. I'm not sure why the Master of Suspense has agreed to do my interview, nor if he'll stay for the duration.

He inserts his chubby hand in mine, briefly.

"Permit me to ask a few questions?"

"Please do."

A curvy blonde carrying a tray of drinks walks by. Hitchcock checks his watch.

"Forgive me, but it's been said you have a 'thing' for blondes?"

"Perhaps it's because they remind me of my mother."

"Lovely woman, was she?"

"Not at all. Quite overbearing, actually. Frightening. She was the type one could subject to MURder."

"Murder your own *mother*?"

"Mothers can be so meddling and invasive, can't they? Messy business, though, murder. Scissors are best."

He eyes a plate of bonbons across the counter and motions to the waitress.

"How about brunettes? Aren't there just as many beautiful brunette actresses as blonde?"

"Mustn't trust a brunette. Too intelligent."

"I'm brunette. You seem to trust me."

Thanking the waitress, he sets the plate of bonbons between us with a crooked smile.

"Which blonde was your favorite: Janet Leigh? Tippi Hedren? Eva Marie Saint? Kim Novak? Grace Kelly? Ingrid Bergman?"

Hitchcock, eyebrows raised, lowers his voice, leans in.

"I suppose I did have a *thing*, as you say, for that icy trollop, Tippi Hedren. You remind me of her in a way, you know."

"Icy trollop? Her career was ruined, thanks to you! I heard she wouldn't dance with you, that night in Tribeca. . ."

Deadpan delivery: "The woman was nobody. No gratitude whatsoever."

"Could it be that your corpulence disgusted her? Tippi, I mean."

Hitchcock addresses me with half-closed eyes:

"Women are not tortured nearly enough in films." He checks my décolleté, then asks: "Have you ever considered going blonde, my dear?"

"Not really," I say, adjusting my top. "Women not tortured enough in films? It wasn't torture enough to put Tippi in a corner and have a trainer throw birds at her until she bled?"

"Ah. *The Birds.* Horrific scene. She enjoyed it, you know..."

"Why the cruelty? Why the blonde fetish?"

"I never said all actors are cattle; I said all actors should be treated like cattle."

"To achieve what?"

"Suspense, my dear. Devise a sinister character, torture the innocent ones; let them all simmer in the same pot. Add a Macguffin, a few plot turns, there you have it. I aim to shock, you see. Gives them pleasure, you know - the same pleasure they have when they wake up from a nightmare. The audience, I mean."

I reach for my cigarettes.

"D'you know how suspense is transmuted?" he asks, picking at a cuticle.

I fumble with my lighter, Hitchcock snatches it and lights my cigarette.

"Imagine I'm filming a man who is leaving his house and he is taking a taxi to catch a train. On the way he says to the taxi driver: "Step on it, man, otherwise I'll never make that train!" The audience will squirm with worry about his fate… D'you see?"

What does happen to the man? I'm wondering, but continue,

"Mr. Hitchcock—I understand you coined the term

Macguffin. **What exactly is it?"**

"Do you like suspense?" he asks, leaning in too close.

"Of course."

"Then you mustn't ask what a Macguffin is, but rather what it *does.*"

"Like the search for uranium in *Notorius*?"

He leans back, pops another bonbon into his mouth.

"Could we get back to the blondes? Grace Kelly? Why wasn't she tortured in *Rear Window*?"

"Quite a frigid trollop, wasn't she?"

"Elegant woman. Was she very influential in your social circles, Mr. Hitchcock?"

"Do call me Hitch. She *was* a real lady, quite. And a whore in the bedroom."

He motions his head toward the two angelic waitresses behind the bar. "Which would you say is more my type?"

"The one with the red sweater. How would you cast her?"

"Perfect victim," he says. "Psychologically damaged, chronically repressed, a bit like Marni. Did you notice her pearls? Blondes make the best victims. They're like virgin snow that shows up the bloody footprints."

I'm nearly out of cigarettes at this point, and turn to scan the room for a vending machine. When I turn back around to face him, Hitchcock is gone. I shrug, down my martini and light a cigarette. The match shakes. I raise my index finger and give a nod to the waitresses behind the bar.

A fat man in a hat carrying a double-bass hobbles by, nearly running into my waitress.

Drink in hand I return to my notes, marking recurring

themes. Suddenly it occurs to me: Had Hitch ever directed *Andy Warhol?* Warhol *could* have appeared in a cameo scene disguised as a blonde. Maybe that was Monroe. I wonder if I'll ever get to finish my interview, and resolve to contact his agent.

Suddenly, Hitch reappears.

"I had to pee."

"Understandable. A few more questions before you disappear again?"

"My pleasure." He smiles, charmingly, waving a hand.

"Marilyn Monroe never appeared in any of your films. Why?"

"Too overtly sexual, even for a blonde."

"You want your blondes to smolder *beneath* the surface?"

"Suspense, my dear, is key. Sex appeal must be indirect. Are you sure you'd never go blonde?"

"Why no throw-away blondes in *Strangers On a Train*? Why all those unlikely casting choices? Next to Ruth Roman, your daughter Patricia looked a bit... awkward."

"How d'you mean?"

"With her thick glasses and precocious speech—wasn't she a little too nerdy?"

"I find nerds attractive. Kim Novak, for example."

"Another blonde. Kim Novak was beautiful in *Vertigo*, but it's true she looked kind of frumpy in those wool suits."

"Are you quite finished, my dear? I'm filming, you know."

"One final question. Your meeting with Francois Truffaut was legendary. Is there any other artist you'd like to meet?"

"R. Mutt."

"Marcel Duchamp?"

"Quite so. Master of the Macguffin, you see."

"Perhaps, later. But first..."

The green light blinks on.

"We hope you've enjoyed tonight's program. Until next time. . . "

Hitchcock's silhouette exits, stage left.

VINCENT & GAUGUIN

"No one has ever written, painted, sculpted, modeled, built, or invented except literally to get out of hell. "
– Antonin Artaud
from *Van Gogh, The Man Suicided by Society*

STUDIO OF THE SOUTH

How long did you and Gauguin live together in Arles?

V: Nine weeks.

Wasn't he meant to live and work with you for at least a year there?

V: It was winter; cold weather kept us closely confined to the little yellow house.

Meaning?

V: We each have big personalities. We needed space to paint. Eventually, serious time apart became necessary.

What did the two of you do when not confined to Yellow House?

V: Made excursions to cafes, galleries, brothels; had disagreements.

About art?

V: Esthetics, mainly. I was more of a realist and worked more quickly.

Gauguin was often considered a Symbolist. Was he as influential as they say regarding your work?

V: G knew about color; he encouraged me to paint from memory, intuition. I had great respect for his talent, but frankly, God spoke through me.

He did say that sunlight emanated from your brush strokes.

V: Who, Gauguin, or God?

I meant Gauguin.

V: I was thinking of Theo. We lived together in Paris.

Is that where you dreamt up the idea about founding an artist's commune in Arles?

V: Right.

Theo never left you, whereas Gauguin did.

V: Devoted brother. He paid our bills.

G: I had a bad feeling about Arles from the beginning.

EXPENSES & DISORDER

You and Gauguin shared expenses at Arles?

G: Expenses? Ha!

V: In exchange for our paintings, Theo sent 250 francs a month to Arles. The paintings were to be sold in Theo's atelier in Paris.

G: The money was kept in a wooden box, where we were to track expenses with a pencil on a piece of paper.

V: Gauguin's idea, not mine.

G: Vincent kept records the way he kept tubes of paint, as you can imagine. Our money was soon squandered on his *hygienic excursions!*

You yourself didn't frequent brothels?

G: Only when absolutely necessary.

SUNFLOWERS

These were iconic. How did you begin?

V: Half a dozen color studies in yellow to capture the light; the first one (yellow on yellow) went in Gauguin's room.

You decorated Gauguin's room with Sunflowers?

V: To brighten things up.

After returning to Paris, Gauguin requested this painting?

V: As if nothing had happened between us. I refused to send it.

What did you think of Gauguin's painting of you, painting Sunflowers?

V: It made me appear like a madman.

RAZOR

Why did you try to murder Gauguin, not once, but twice?

V: I disliked his painting of me painting Sunflowers.

NIGHT CAFE

You and Gauguin both painted *les poulets* at the *Night Cafe*? Gauguin admired Arlesian women?

V: Only as subjects. G preferred his women primitive. I told him his poulets lacked feeling.

Whereas you captured their suffering.

V: Their suffering was my own.

Is that why you painted the *café* in reds, greens, and yellows?

V: There, "one could destroy oneself, go mad, or commit a crime," I liked to say.

G: I should never have bought him that second absinthe.

EAR

Your ear: Did you sever the entire ear, or just the tip?

V: Ask Gauguin.

G: It was cut close to the head.

V: How do you know?

G: Rachel, the prostitute, said so.

V: Did she like me?

G: She didn't care much for the bloody ear, delivered in an envelope.

There's a rumor that it was Gauguin who cut off your ear with his épée during a lovers quarrel. Is that true?

V: [shrugs]

G: [Turns away]

TAHITI

[To V] **I'm sorry about the ear-question.**

V: Buy me another absinthe; I may forgive you.

[To G] **Tahiti: Why?**

G: To remove myself from the company of imbeciles. To write. To paint.

What is it about *les primitives* that captivated you?

G: Their natural beauty and complete innocence; unlike *les poulets*.

Why marry a 13 year old Tahitian girl, rather than a prostitute?

G: [shrugs] I loved her.

[To V] **Your opinion on G leaving his wife and children in Paris to move to Tahiti and marry a 13 year old girl?**

V: [shrugs] *G was always leaving somebody.*

PAINTINGS

Prior to Gauguin's arrival, you painted solo inside the Studio of the South?

V: It took several months before G agreed to come. In the meantime I created "The Poet's Garden" in anticipation of his arrival.

A series depicting the view of the gardens across from Gauguin's room. What else?

V: Half a dozen versions of "Sunflowers," my own bedroom, the fields and dusty roads of Arles, Provence; Yellow House; the Night Café.

Some of your most beloved paintings were painted at Arles.

V: Yes.

COOKING

Who did the cooking in Yellow House if you couldn't go out?

G: I did.

V: I once made a soup, but G refused to eat it.

G: V's soup was unpalatable; afterwards he ran around, shouting: *La casquette au père Daudet!* *

THE ALTRUISM OF THE GOSPEL

In winter, 1886 you sold the painting "Pink Shrimps" for 5 francs so you could eat, then, upon encountering the outstretched palm of a Parisienne beggar woman outside the salon, you promptly deposited the coin straight into it.

---

* From *Gauguin's Intimate Journals*, by Paul Gauguin

V: Where did you hear that?

Gauguin made note of it in his journal.

G: Later, the painting sold for 500 francs at auction.

FORGIVENESS

[To V] **Thoughts on Gauguin's untimely departure, immediately following *the ear incident*?**

V: I forgive him, mostly.

[To G] **Describe your impression after nine weeks with Vincent in Arles?**

G: I'm still haunted by the experience.

ASYLUM

You never visited Vincent in Saint Rémy or any other hospital?

G: He was consumed with his painting at the time.

He wrote to you about it?

G: He had hopes of recovering soon and visiting Brittany.

[To V] **What happened?**

V: *I had epileptic seizures. In between seizures I could paint.*

You wanted out of the asylum?

V: *You mean, The Penal Colony?*

Eventually, finally, you were released and reached your wheat fields?

V: I took my easel, camp stool, yellow paint and brushes.

What would you say to Gauguin now?

V: I would tell him I love him.

GEORGIA O

"I had to create an equivalent for what I felt about what I was looking at –
not copy it.
– Georgia O'Keeffe

At *Gallery 291*, Alfred Stieglitz introduced the American art world to some of the most avant garde European artists of the time: Matisse, Rodin, Rousseau, Cézanne, Picasso, Brâncuşi, Picabia, and Duchamp. Why would he have singled you out as an artist he wanted to exhibit?

I suppose he liked my hands.

The photos of you, the passionate letters between you and Stieglitz have been well-documented. Do you think they've played a part in your ongoing mystique?

My ongoing what?

The spiritual mystique surrounding you: the erotic photos taken by Stieglitz, your sensual paintings of fruits and flowers, meditative abstracts, bleached desert bones and skulls; landscapes. Bordering the shamanic.

Oh?

Do you see yourself as a visionary?

Not really.

I'd like to address the question of sexual overtones in your early work. Were they intentional?

Not at all. The Freudian business simply began with Stieglitz and my abstracts.

Care to explain?

As you mentioned, he promoted my first solo exhibit in his gallery, "291," where my black and white charcoals were immediately interpreted as sexual. From then on, critics considered everything I did to be manifestations of female sexuality no matter whether representational or abstract, color or black and white.

Could your exhibit have had to do with sexuality subconsciously?

If sexuality is expressed in color, pattern, form, and light; well, yes.

What about your flowers? Flowers aren't necessarily sexual, but somehow yours evoke...

I paint Nature as I see it.

You seem to have gotten very close to your subjects.

God is in the details.

Many of your large-scale renderings, such as the flowers, are remarkable hybrids that blur the lines between realism and abstraction. How did you manage to combine the two so sensuously?

Years of practice.

But then you decided to unlearn what you'd been taught, and go your own way, with Stieglitz's help, of course?

[G. shrugs]

You worked in the era of the Surrealists. Did you ever care to join them?

I dislike chauvinistic groups with agendas.

You weren't inspired by Surrealism's erotic imagery, esotericism and mystery?

Sometimes, my dear, a cigar is just a cigar.

Not even Man-Ray? Weren't you influenced by Modernist photography?

Man-Ray had his moments.

So, what was the attraction between you and Stieglitz? Wasn't he twenty-something years older?

Twenty-three. It was he who was smitten with me from the beginning.

He was first enamored with your early charcoal abstracts, right? What was next?

Alchemy. New York. Lake George. New Mexico.

By "alchemy" you must mean your "chemistry" with Stieglitz. Critics say in some photos you completely opened up before his camera. With such a strong connection between you two, why move to New Mexico?

The high desert is vast and beautiful, don't you agree?

A few of my favorites, "Black Door with Snow, 1955," "Patio Door with Green Leaf, 1956," as well as "In the Patio VIII, 1950," were painted soon after you settled in New Mexico. The heaviness of dense architectural forms, shapes, shadows, contrasting with the lightness of snow, falling leaves, hints of color: was the Zen quality intentional?

I'm capturing stillness.

Was there a connection between your Ghost Ranch home in the high desert and the Wisconsin prairies? Wasn't it on a dairy farm that you grew up?

Think of it this way: Peace derived from simplicity = a

vastness of space.

If one's a recluse, I suppose. The rumors that Stieglitz had an affair with an even younger woman after you became famous: Are they true? Was that the reason you went to New Mexico?

No.

Even though he left his first wife for you, then left you for another woman?

I don't know.

Are the desert scenes shamanic, are the flowers sexual; why didn't you and Stieglitz have children?

Next question.

You were born in 1887, the same year Van Gogh went to Arles; you lived to be almost 99. Care to share your secret to longevity?

Being left in peace.

Could your long life have had something to do with the young apprentice you hired at age 86, Juan Hamilton? Rumor has it he was 60 years younger and you left him all your money....

Could be, I'm not sure.

And at 96, you thought you married him?

Didn't I?

The young potter was already married, yet he brought his wife and two children to live in your home even after you signed over your estate and power of attorney to him.

I invited them.

You weren't celebrating a wedding as he led you to believe; you were signing a will. Your family sued. Juan won. Then he compromised.

Well, he kept my art and my secrets safe for a small fee, so I didn't mind.

Final question? Both you and Louise Bourgeois lived to age 98 employing male assistants who were 50 to 60 years younger. Was that due to sensuality or to your artistic personas?

Louise Bourgeois? Isn't she the one famous for spiders? Ask *her*.

LOUISE B

"To unravel a torment you have to begin somewhere."
— Louise Bourgeois

Let us get something clear before we begin. In general I don't need an interview to clarify my thoughts. It is absurd, a pain in the neck! Interviews are a process of clarification of other people's thoughts, not mine. In fact I always have to know more about you than you know about me. All the same I like to be crystal clear when I speak. I like to be a glass house. There is no mask in my work. Therefore, as an artist, all I can share with other people is this transparency. *

Frankly, I'm a little intimidated by you.

What are you afraid of?

I suppose confronting you and your work is to confront my own fears.

All the more reason to begin.

Like Georgia O'Keeffe, your work is sometimes sexual in nature, although you tend to be more direct.

I've never met Ms. O'Keeffe, but her work only skirts around sex. For me, it's best to be direct. I don't like keeping secrets.

Interestingly, both you and O'Keeffe lived to be 98 and employed male apprentices who were decades younger. Juan Hamilton assisted O'Keeffe and Jerry Gorovoy was

---

* from *Louise Bourgeois*. Robert Storr and Paulo Herkenhoff. Phaidon Press (2003).

your assistant, right?

Jerry and I worked closely for 30 years. Our relationship was complex.

Gorovoy has written that you were jealous and possessive. That you fell apart every time he left to install your work, and punished him when he returned, to the point that he felt guilty for leaving.

Where are you going with these questions?

Can we talk about your career? You met so many prominent artists: Bacon, Duchamp, Miró, De Kooning. Yet compared to them you received little recognition. Did you feel slighted by the official art world?

My body of work speaks for itself. Without it, I'm miserable, so to answer your question, I suppose it wouldn't matter if I were more famous or not.

Did it seem likely that your giant spiders would be the work for which you're best known?

The spiders don't tell the whole story, of course, but nearly anybody can relate to them. As to what they represent, that is up to the viewer.

In your case they're symbolic of Mother?

Mother, fragility, entrapment.

Your other work is full of cells, cages, or encapsulated figures.

Sex, betrayal, and love are forms of entrapment.

Eroticism and pain, ambiguously morphing sexual organs. What's that about?

It's about getting at the truth. Confronting one's demons, one's sexuality, anger and fears—about love, especially.

How are you able to get so close to those elusive concepts?

Artists must get close to them, otherwise there's only surface and no substance.

But most people don't like to look at their fears, anger, and pain. Some don't want to acknowledge their own sexuality.

That's the role of an artist. To illuminate what's hidden so that viewers may take a peek into the darkness they're avoiding.

Even if it means creating something unappealing?

Of course.

You were born and raised in France, yet you call the United States home?

I've lived in the United States for over 30 years.

Would you call yourself a patriot?

I'm a French-American artist.

What was your childhood like, in France?

When I was growing up, my English governess lived with us. She was my father's mistress for more than ten years. Imagine! After a night of love-making, the two of them sat across from us at the breakfast table.

Your mother knew?

He began the affairs when she was sick with influenza. She turned a blind eye, enduring multiple affairs. In those days, divorce wasn't an option—French men behaved as they pleased.

How did you feel about it?

Take a look at my work.

How did you come to study art? Was your father supportive?

Never. He was, in fact, opposed.

Yet you've won several awards, taught at prominent universities, you have a bio a mile long. Was gaining your father's approval important?

Not at all.

How do the spiders represent "Mother"?

When I think of spiders, I think of industriousness, protection, self-defense, fragility.

The spiders are called "Ode a ma mere." Yet, they are towering - as tall as buildings.

My mother was my best friend. Like a spider, she was a weaver. My family was in the business of tapestry restoration, and mother was in charge of the workshop. Like spiders, my mother was very clever. Spiders are friendly presences that eat mosquitoes. We know that mosquitoes spread diseases and are therefore unwanted. So, spiders are helpful and protective, just like my mother.

What are the cells about? Are you making statements about art as well as personal statements?

My work is completely autobiographical. I make the exploration of identity the purpose of my art. I believe in taking art out of the frame and making it front and center. It's about identity while looking at form, while looking at culture in a broader sense.

A criticism of culture, perhaps?

A criticism of culture's obsession with the "Now," i.e., the young. Modernism's refusal to refer to the past...I am rejecting this refusal by looking at my own past...

A past some would find difficult to bear...hence, the cells?

Inside the cell, I can both articulate my helplessness and violation, and also control it.

Can your cells also represent "biological cells"?

Consider the way we look at animals in cages, both with a sense of wonder and sadness and entrapment. The industrial cages contain mementos of my childhood, symbols of my torment as a child. When they say I should get over it, here is my response.

What is the best part about being an artist?

An artist can show things that other people are terrified of expressing.

Which artist would you recommend I interview next?

That's your problem. There is always Man Ray.

MAN RAY

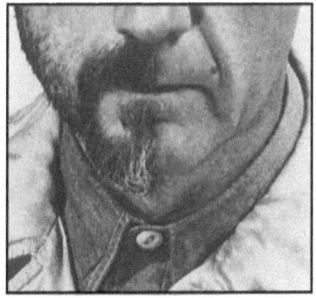

"I like contradictions. We have never attained the infinite variety of contradictions that exist in nature. Tomorrow I shall contradict myself. That is one way I have of asserting my liberty, the real liberty which one does not find as a member of society."
– Man Ray

You've said you prefer—you *require* a certain autonomy or freedom in order to work? What exactly *is* this freedom?

My work, as well as my personality, defies definition; therefore, having this discussion seems pointless. On the other hand, it is very important to discuss art. At least, it is important to discuss art in general.

Do you mean to say that art that occurs by chance or generated without pre-planning or preconception is more "free" than other kinds of art?

The element of the unexpected is favorable, yes, however, my ideas about autonomy and freedom convey much more than a general synopsis of my work.

So, I'm assuming a discussion of attributes such as "stylistic identity," would be vehemently rejected?

I don't believe in linear progression, advancement, development, or consistency in creating a work of art. An artist must go his own way, wherever it may lead.

Is this Dada?

Is what Dada?

Our discussing and not discussing art simultaneously.

We can discuss my work, if you like, and we can discuss art in general. But I would rather not discuss my work and art in general at the same time.

I think I understand. Here's a different approach. What would you like to say about contemporary art and its use (or non-use) of technology? How would *you* use it?

Technology is abhorrent to humanity. Any found object may contain a kind of inherent poetry and can evoke a sense of mystery, given sufficient imagination and intelligence. I would leave art up to chance and up to the receiver. Turn mistakes into art; call them by droll and witty names.

Like your *Cadeau, 1921* or your *Object to Be Destroyed, 1923*? *Contraption, 1944*? *Trompe L'Oeuf, 1963* [a photograph featuring a large white plastic ball wedged inside a toilet seat]?

Why not?

What purpose might these found "mistakes," these poetic, *objets d'art* serve?

None whatsoever; unless you find purpose or meaning in art or, conversely, anti-art. I want to facilitate questions, to illustrate them; to communicate via whatever means possible, without restriction.

So, what's the point?

The point is, not to be caught up in having a point.

Then, where does technology fit in?

Technology fits in with the rest of humanity. Full-steam ahead.

Can we move on? I'd like to discuss your friends and lovers.

As long as you don't hold them against me.

You employed models such as Kiki de Montparnasse and Meret Oppenheim to pose in some of your most famous photographs. Did they also become your lovers?

Oh, no, I only photographed them.

Nude, and in erotic poses?

In black and white. Sometimes they were posed as musical instruments. Like sculptures.

Meret Oppenheim was an emerging artist then. Did you help her career along?

Indirectly, yes. Her fur teacup was actually Picasso's idea. The idea came to him one day when the two of them were having coffee in Paris.

Ah, Picasso. Ladies' man. Frequenter of cafes. The "Déjeuner en Fourriere" was his idea?

Yes. Meret Oppenheim designed jewelry as well as sculpture. Didn't you know?

And Kiki? She was your Muse for many years.

She was a Muse to many men, or so my wife would say. Wonderful model.

You were best known for photography, yet you were a prolific painter, sculptor, filmmaker and writer, employing various modes of execution in each field. Do you have

comments about your approach to technique?

I consider myself a painter first and foremost. I got into photography in order to be able to paint.

Would you say that painting allowed you the most creative freedom? Was it for you the most expressive medium?

Painting is more organic, but again, consistency is not an issue with me, and my approach to each piece is different, whatever the medium.

What engages you most when making art?

A work of art which can be taken apart and put together as if it was some kind of machine holds no interest for me. What does engage my interest in a work of art are those facets which defy analysis and are imbued with mystery. This applies to my own efforts as well as to the creations of others.

So, your technique is actually about not having a technique?

Emphasis on technique may cloud ideas, or else conceal the artist's impoverishment of ideas. Germinal Ideas must only be interesting in some way. In whatever form [my work] is finally presented, by a drawing, by a painting, by a photograph, or by the object itself in its original materials and dimensions, it is designed to amuse, bewilder, annoy or to inspire reflection, but not to arouse admiration for any technical excellence usually sought for in works of art. The streets are full of admirable craftsmen, but so few are practical dreamers.*

Your friendship with Marcel Duchamp lasted decades. What was the connection between you two?

Dada, perhaps. Anti-art.

---

* from *Man Ray.* Jules Langsner. Los Angeles County Museum of Art, Lytton Gallery, 1966.

Your friend Hans Richter wrote that you had strange eating habits and that you are "always the same unobtrusively – pessimistic optimist who can handle life, women, finances, art dealers, American businessmen, and visiting firemen just as expertly as [you do] photography and painting." Do you agree?

[Man Ray shrugs]

Do you have any other comments about art-making?

Art simply varies in its sources of inspiration and in its modes of execution. It can vary within one man, depending on his curiosity and his sense of freedom...The real experiment is in proportion to the desire to discover and enjoy, and this desire alone can be the only measure of the painter's value to the rest of society.*

Isn't Dada just a bunch of pseudo-intellectual nonsense?

Ask Duchamp.

---

* from *Man Ray* by Jules Langsner. Los Angeles County Museum of Art, Lytton Gallery, 1966.

DUCHAMP

"*Dada is this; Dada is that; Dada is this; Dada is that;
Dada is nevertheless shit.*"
– Tristan Tzara

"*Lechecs, c'est moi.*"
– Marcel Duchamp

Here we are, Monsieur Duchamp.

So kind of you to invite me.

Actually, I've been avoiding you.

Avoiding me? Why?

Interviewing you presents a challenge. It is a turning point in the book.

Oh?

When things get serious.

How could things be getting serious if you are interviewing me?

That's what concerns me.

Come again?

I'm afraid to ask the wrong questions for fear of creating a farce.

Questions, such as?

Who are you, and what exactly are you up to?

I'm not sure I know what you mean?

Art.

I am not up to anything serious, if that helps.

Yet, people still look to you for inspiration. Everything in contemporary art comes down to you.

You mustn't count on me. I'm unreliable.

Ok, but I must say, you made quite an impression on me early on.

Really?

You were a rebel. And quite handsome! Some have called you the grandfather of conceptual art.

What a concept!

You have also been called a chameleon.

Because I change colors?

Because you never adhered very long to any particular style or genre.

That's true, I suppose.

Upon graduating from art school you practiced a variety of styles, including Cubism, Symbolism, Fauvism, and popular illustration. Did you favor any particular style over the other?

I took a little of this, a little of that; perhaps I favored them all at one time or another. All and none of those styles seriously influenced me.

You come from a large family of artists. Seven children.

C'est vrai.

Gaston, Raymond, Suzanne, etc. Even your parents and grandparents were artists.

Also true.

And after art school?

I spent my life going back and forth between France and the U.S., making art, causing scandals.

You began with painting, causing a scandal at Salon des Indépendents in 1912 and then scandalized them again at the Armory Show in 1913, with your painting "Nude Descending a Staircase."

Indeed. Here I was satirizing Cubism to a degree, which was not well received.

Still, you must have been somewhat engaged with Cubism and Surrealism, and of course Dada and chess...

I took none of it seriously.

Except chess.

And Dada.

We mustn't forget the readymades you began making in 1914.

Antidotes to retinal art.

Can you explain?

The curious thing about the readymade is that I've never been able to arrive at a definition or explanation that fully satisfies me.

But surely worth mentioning here?

I'm not at all sure that the concept of the readymade isn't the most important single idea to come out of my work.

The urinal signed R. Mutt: You had it anonymously shipped to the Salon des Independents with no explanation.

Organized exhibitions irritate me. I wanted to have a little fun!

You submitted your "urinal" as a piece of art, not intending that it be taken seriously?

I wanted to see if others would take the bait and struggle with the problem of creating labels.

A challenge to the establishment?

It was, of course, just for fun.

You were among the founding members of the *Société des Indépendents*, yet preferred not to play by the rules.

I prefer to turn the rules on their heads. In fact, let's change the rules of this very interview.

How?

An interview is a series of questions and answers, no? We might ask ourselves why.

In my case, the interview is to get a sense of the artist's personality, and to record him in his own words.

Perhaps what is needed to get a sense of the artist's thoughts and personality is for him to conduct the interview himself.

You mean, the artist is in control?

Or, out of control. That is what I propose. Something like that.

But suppose that makes me uncomfortable?

Let us both relinquish control, and see what develops naturally.

I'll try. *Je suis d'accord.* [I said that to Duchamp, but was really thinking, "WTF?"]

We might not even need to ask questions or provide answers. We could just have a chat. Coffee?

Thank you. By the way, what did you think of my interview with your friend, Man Ray?

Rather stiff, I'm afraid. He's much more congenial than you depicted him.

It may be necessary to change the rules again with him.

I always disagree with the rules.

Shall we make new rules?

That does not sound appealing.

And impose constraints?

Shouldn't I interview you?

Go ahead, then.

You said this interview was a turning point for you. What did you mean?

I suppose I meant I never thought I would get this far.

Writing a book of interviews? But that should be easy.

Easy for you to say, the grandfather of Conceptual Art. You spent your entire life working on "The Large Glass." You must understand that complexity takes time.

The Glass is not complex. Just layered.

I would hope it is the same with this book.

I'm sure it will be. You've asked good questions!

I'd like to ask about *Étant donnés*, your last major work. The art world thought you had given up art for chess...

I worked secretly on the piece from 1946 to 1966 in my Greenwich Village studio.

Some might argue this piece to be your masterpiece, even more so than "Glass."

I've thought a good deal about relationships and about give and take. I suppose that was inherent in "Large Glass."

And sex. And compromise. Time, and space? These are apparent themes in *Étant donnés*.

The naked woman with her face hidden, holding the gas lamp against an urban landscape backdrop is an universal image, I think.

You used two different models for the figure.

Yes. My girlfriend's body and my second wife's arm.

And the medium?

It is composed of an old wooden door, nails, bricks, brass, aluminum sheet, steel binder clips, velvet, leaves, twigs, a female form made of parchment, hair, glass, plastic clothespins, oil paint, linoleum, an assortment of lights, a landscape composed of hand-painted and photographed elements and an electric motor housed in a cookie tin which rotates a perforated disc.

Amazing!

I knew what I was doing.

You mean…?

I had it all planned.

Your last work of art?

C'est ça, oui.

Your last statement.

It may have been confusing, but that was not my intention.

The door with the peep holes through which the piece must be viewed is a little confusing.

The piece has an instruction manual.

I thought you were against imposing rules?

I am. Except when they are my own.

Are there rules in Dada, or Surrealism?

Consider this little experiment a bit of surrealism and then tell me.

Experiment?

This essay of yours.

I don't understand.

Today, my dear, we've created a new readymade. Signed with a flourish by yours truly!

I should have known...

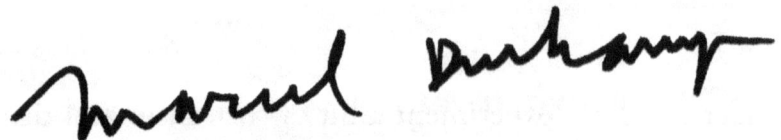

DALÍ

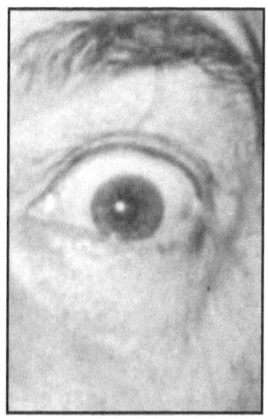

"Le Surréalisme, c'est moi."

"Every morning when I wake up, I experience an exquisite joy — the joy of being Salvador Dalí — and I ask myself in rapture: What wonderful things is this Salvador Dalí going to accomplish today?"

– Salvador Dalí

Dalí, is it really you?

Indeed, it is, who else, but who?

I thought this might be an illusion.

I never wished to cause confusion.

So, what about those melting clocks?

Nightmares, as I stroked my fox.

May we begin the interview?

My dear, but that is up to you!

Tell me, you were born in Spain?

In Catalonia, in the rain.

Figueras, isn't that the name?

My childhood was fraught with pain.

The reason for your painted dreams?

Lions were tormenting me!

Freudian, of course, in nature.

Insects, gruesome headless creatures!

Your painted dreams and memories?

My enemies were after me…

Pathological distortions, visions?

I'm never good at big decisions.

Salvador, your older brother?

He died, and it destroyed my mother.

Your parents named you after him?

I was his reincarnation!

Good, we've stopped rhyming.

It is just as well.

Why is that? Don't you think I could have sustained it?

You could have gone on infinitely if DALÍ were to help you.

Perhaps. I suppose, though, it was only a matter of Time.

Time is relative, my dear.

Not fixed?

Certainly not.

You mean, clocks. Einstein's theory of relativity?

DALÍ's theory!

You met Freud once, I read, and he privately called you a fanatic.

I was delighted!

***Are* you a fanatic?**

I am a Surrealist!

Didn't the Surrealists expel you formally from their group in 1934?

Why should they do that?

Your political ambiguity, your refusal to denounce fascism, your unapologetic support of the Spanish monarchy.

Surrealism can exist in an apolitical context, I maintain.

You mean to tell me you don't believe art and politics are inextricably linked? The Surrealists expelled you formally!

I myself am Surrealism!

You've been criticized for making too much money and causing scenes with your extravagant behavior.

But I enjoy extravagance! Money is necessary to live, no?

Did you sell out, Dalí? May I call you Dalí?

I prefer to be called Salvador!

Salvador?

The Savior!

Rescuer?

It is I, perhaps, who was rescued.

By Gala?

My wife, my muse of 50 years.

And there were no other muses?

There may have been one or two…

Younger ones, I bet. But Gala was your primary inspiration. At least in the beginning. Especially in the beginning.

How do you think I came up with "The Great Masturbator?"

She was ten years your senior, and married to Surrealist writer Paul Éluard when you met?

I was tormented with desire! What do you think my paintings are about!?

I heard your father disapproved?

He was Catholic.

How long were you together?

DALÍ was married to Gala for 50 years!

But didn't she try to poison you in the end?

She was putting medication in my tea. She did not know better!

She was semi-senile.

Who can tell the difference? Sanity? Senility?

She was your great love.

I bought her a castle in the 1970s.

And your father eventually accepted her when you returned to Spain?

Eventually we were married in the Catholic Church.

You denounced Surrealism for Catholicism?

I am Catalonian! I was baptized Catholic!

I also heard an Italian friar performed an exorcism on you, and you gave him a special crucifix that you had made just for him.

It is true. From then on, I was saved.

Tell me about your early work. You were influenced by Velázquez, Miró, Picasso?

Geniuses!

You were also friends with Lorca.

Not in *that* way!

Such talented fellow countrymen. What about Luis Bunuel?

No more about Buñuel!

What happened? You two split? But the two of you made those Surrealist films, right? *Un Chien Andalou* **(1929***), L'Age D'or* **(1930)? What did you do? He was the filmmaker.**

DALÍ should not have to explain!

I heard you wrote the scripts. Is there nothing you don't do? Drawing, painting, film, sculpture, fashion, photography, jewelery? Cubism, Dada, Surrealism…

DALÍ is multi-talented!

In your early paintings you referred to Flemish Art, the Italian Renaissance, and even had encountered Impressionism, Neo-Impressionism, and Fauvism.

I disagree with formalism.

Sounds like Man Ray! You attended the Academy of Fine Arts in Madrid in 1921.

All artists should have a good background.

There is so much more to ask. For example, I noticed that you frequently used familiar objects as a point of departure in your early work...Watches, insects, pianos, telephones, old prints, other animals, imparting to them fetishistic significance.

Blood! Decay! Excrement! I painted as a madman (before I was exorcised) in a continuous frenzy of induced paranoia!

You used "microscopic realism" to objectify the dream world.

Trompe-l'oeil as well!

You used this technique to make your dream world more tangibly real than observed nature?

Hand-painted dream photographs, I call them!

Why do you use an exclamation mark after every sentence?

I am DALÍ!

What about symbolism in your work? Time, Elephants, Eggs, Ants, Snails, Locusts...What are these all about?

Desire, Hope, Love, Fertility, Sexual Anxiety, Death, Decay, the human head, Waste, and Fear!

Oh, Salvador, that is quite a lot to wrap my head around.

But you did not ask the most important question of DALÍ!

What's that?

What song was playing when he died?

Could it have been *Tristan and Isolde*?

How did you know?

It is well known. You died in your Theater Museum, three blocks from the house in which you were born.

You have included almost everything about DALÍ.

One last question: which artist would you suggest I interview next?

Do you know Madge Gill?

The outsider artist and medium?

Precisely. She is the one DALÍ would suggest.

Would you settle for Leonora Carrington?

CARRINGTON

"I painted for myself...I never believed anyone would exhibit or buy my work."
— Leonora Carrington

Journal Entry

I'm currently institutionalized. On my birthday, my family decided it best to cart me off to Spain, placing me here. I would have preferred to stay in Saint-Martin-d'Ardèche, keeping my cats with me, and all my things. In my room in the south I had been saving my cats' hair from their brushes in order to spin it into yarn for knitting scarves. I hadn't quite saved up enough hair, but I had 4 jars full. I had a red hen that laid an egg once a day on my pillow. I kept him in the backyard. I had brown glass jars of (mostly dried up) potions from my friend Carmella who knew about herbs and was clairvoyant. She, like me, painted surrealist scenes, mainly female-themed, often egg-centric, and dealing with domesticity. I knew Carmella in Paris, before the war, before I met Max, but it wasn't until we were both living in Mexico that we became close friends. One day we were sitting in her kitchen, reading tea leaves, when the red hen spoke to us...

Excuse me, Leonora?

Yes?

Sorry to interrupt, but may I ask a few questions?

What about?

What are you writing?

This is an excerpt from a fictitious journal entry that I used in one of my books.

"The Hearing Trumpet"?

That's it. How did you know?

I've been reading it. I was surprised to learn that you were a prolific writer as well as painter.

Oh, yes.

You wrote several books?

Nine, I think.

What's this one about?

It's about an old woman, Marian Letherby, who distrusts people (especially her family) and communicates with animals.

Was she very old?

Ninety-two.

You were quite young when you wrote it. How did you come to make your protagonist so old?

Marian at ninety-two represents a connection to a past that dates as far back as witches have existed. I like to call her my crone-like muse because her wisdom inspires me.

Reminds me of Bréton and the Surrealists' study of witches.

You mean "La Sorcière," Michelet's study of witches?

André Bréton was enamored with Michelet's text, wasn't he?

Indeed. He associated Michelet's view of a witch's creative powers with the female muse, later adopted by the male Surrealists.

A feminist notion, isn't it? I mean, the "witch" as a

persona for the powerful and independent woman, as an antithesis to the male Surrealist notion of female muse as mere trophy?

I suppose so.

Are you a witch?

Oh, well…some say my studio is quite magical.

I've heard your studio called "the most dream-saturated place I know." Others have called it "the den of a 16th century magician." How do you respond?

I'm a dreamer, that's true, and magic, well, it's in part what I try to invoke. An escape, I suppose.

You first fled to in Mexico in 1942?

Yes, it turned out to be a magical place for me, but not at first.

You were fleeing institutionalization in Spain and the

scrutiny of your family after your release?

Right. Mexico was a new world after all I had endured during the war.

André Breton called it "the Surrealist place par excellence."

Oh? It was, I suppose. Still, I missed England with its scented gardens, cherry trees, its meadows; the song of the thrush…

Who comprised your core group of friends in Mexico?

European Surrealist exiles, mainly. My second husband, Cziki Weisz (a Hungarian photographer) and I spent most of our time with the poet Benjamin Péret and his artist wife, Remedios Varo.

You became very close with Varo, another Surrealist, yet you didn't associate much with Octavio Paz, Frida Kahlo and Diego Rivera, prominent artists who were also there?

We knew them, but weren't the closest of friends. Remedios Varo and I were kindred spirits. Together we explored Surrealism, alchemy, and art.

In your kitchen, right?

Her kitchen and mine served as laboratories for concocting various recipes that were eventually served to our friends at parties. The Mexican markets where the Curanderas bought ingredients such as herbs and roots for their curative soups inspired us. We were interested in the symbolism of eggs, for example. The list goes on and on.

You and Remedios Varo both came from Catholic backgrounds. Did you reject Catholicism?

We invented our own hybrid belief system, I suppose.

Meaning?

My mother was Irish. She practiced a kind of hybrid Catholicism that mixed Christian beliefs with Celtic mythology, not seeing them as mutually exclusive systems. She gave me the ability to mix cultural references, and it was this kind of hybrid that influenced what Varo and I explored in our artistic lives.

A kind of alchemy in the kitchen?

Yes, and on the canvas. We both painted using various alchemical themes, as you know.

Can we talk about the writing a bit more? What inspired you to write?

After Max was taken away the second time I wrote "White Rabbits," "Waiting," and "The Seventh Horse." André Bréton suggested I document my experience being institutionalized and severely medicated.

You were given drugs in the asylum?

I was given "convulsive therapy" and treated with the drugs Cardiazol, a powerful anxiolytic drug, and Luminal, a barbiturate.

Did the drugs affect your work?

[LC shrugs].

You mention Max Ernst. He was, of course, your lover when you were twenty, and he was 26 years your senior. It must have been a shock to your parents, undoubtedly?

That's right.

What happened to him?

He was taken away twice, interred in camps. With the out-break of World War II Max, who was German, was arrested by the French authorities for being a "hostile alien." Paul Éluard and other friends interceded, and Max was discharged a few weeks later.

What about the second time?

Soon after the Nazis invaded France, he was arrested again, this time by the Gestapo, because his art was considered by the Nazis to be "degenerate." He managed to escape, but I was left behind.

He fled to America?

Right, with the help of Peggy Guggenheim, whom he later married.

Consequently you had a breakdown when you left France for Spain?

Paralyzing anxiety and increasing delusions culminated in my final breakdown at the British embassy in Madrid. At the time my family and friends thought it best to hospitalize me. I was usually rather uncontrollable, but this time, I was inconsolable.

Your stories often convey a wild and disturbing disquiet. Would you say the very act of writing them was a kind of cathartic purging?

Making art is always useful as catharsis. My stories take place in another realm, similar to my paintings, where, as you know, mythological creatures rather than humans, rule.

You grew up as a débutante and the daughter of well-to-do merchants in England. How did you find yourself in the company of Surrealists in Paris?

I began drawing when I was four. After a series of expulsions from various schools, I was deemed uneducable, so I informed my parents I was going to art school in London.

Were your parents supportive of the idea of you becoming an artist?

My father was not. My mother and I had similar

temperaments. In fact, my mother was also good at drawing. We both loved drawing horses.

You say you were rebellious? How?

I vehemently disliked institutions, and often escaped from them, to the dismay of many of my captors. Freedom was critical to me; I carried that sensibility to the end.

When were you introduced to Surrealism?

I was a newly enrolled art student. When the First International Surrealist Exhibition came to London, my mother, by a strange twist of fate, gave me Herbert Read's book, *Surrealism* (1936), a catalogue of artists from the exhibition that included Bréton's essays and Max Ernst's work.

Were you aware that that very year (1936) Hitler was poised to dispatch Gestapo troops on France that would ultimately arrest all German citizens living in France?

All I knew at the time was that I needed to separate myself from the world of debutant balls and polite society. I felt confined and desperately needed to create. That historically significant events were manifesting all around me was secondary to my urgent need for freedom.

In Paris you moved in the same circles as Bréton, Tanguy, Péret, Belmer, Arp, Picasso and Dalí to name a few. How did you finally meet Max Ernst?

It was 1937 and we were at a party in London. He was notoriously well-liked by women. I was new on the scene and too stubborn to be impressed, although I had been in love with him even before we met. He saw me across the room, and I saw him. Eventually he approached and put his finger in my beer to prevent the foam from overflowing.

He was married at the time, to Dorothea Tanning? I heard she was emotionally volatile.

Yes. She was quite jealous whenever we appeared together in public, often causing scenes with her hysterics.

Ernst separated from Tanning and the two of you moved to Saint-Martin-d'Ardèche in the south? Were you happy there?

Very happy. It was also a very productive time for us, artistically, and a time of growth, especially for me.

After your separation from Max you went to Mexico where you stayed for over thirty years, having two sons

and producing a massive body of work that includes writing, painting, drawing and sculpture. What would you say is your most important work?

It must be "The Inn of the Dawn Horse (Self-Portrait)" from 1939.

Painted during your early days in Paris. Why that particular piece?

I was able to experiment during that time and the experimentation went well. In *Self-Portrait*, I offer my own interpretation of female sexuality by looking toward my own sexual reality rather than theorizing on the subject, as was custom by other Surrealists in the movement.

Were you interpreting Freud here?

Actually, my focus was on magical realism and alchemy. I used autobiographical detail and symbolism as the subjects of my paintings.

Your move away from the characterization of female sexuality subverted the traditional male role of the Surrealist movement, no?

Yes. *Self-Portrait* also offers insight into my interest in the 'alchemical transformation of matter and my response to the Surrealist cult of desire as a source of creative inspiration.' The hyena depicted in *Self-Portrait* joins both male and female into a whole, metaphoric of the worlds of the night and the dream.

A very interesting approach, considering you worked in such a male-dominated arena.

Thank you. I'd like to think my work of the 1940s is focused on the underlying theme of women's role in the creative process.

Were you a member of the feminist faction of Surrealism that made reference to women's roles in the domestic sphere as *les femme-enfants*, objects of male desire, contesting their roles as mere muses to male Surrealist artists? You were both talented and beautiful.

I suppose I used my intelligence to meet all the influential artists, and subsequently make my own contributions to the art world.

Returning to my earlier question, Leonora: do you consider yourself a kind of witch?

A witch? No. A sorceress or alchemist, yes. I suppose I do. practice a kind of magic.

MADGE GILL

"It was in 1919 when I first started my work…I felt that I had an artistic faculty seeking expression…all the time I was in quite a normal state of mind and there was no suggestion of a 'spirit' standing beside me. I simply felt inspired. But I felt I was definitely guided by an unseen force, though I could not say what its actual nature was."
– Madge Gill

You're considered by many to be an outsider artist. Is that an accurate description?

What's that?

It's a term that can mean "self-taught," among other things.

I'd say I'm a visionary and my work is mediumistic.

How is that?

My spirit guide compels me to create; I deliver messages from another realm through my drawings.

Are you saying you're possessed when you draw? When did this begin?

March 3rd, 1920 the medium was taken in a trance and controlled by MYRNINEREST, my spirit guide.

You were thirty-six then?

Yes.

How did all this happen?

My aunt introduced me to spiritualism when I was 19. She held séances and knew a great deal about psychic automatism and its varying degrees.

Is it true that once possessed, producing art became "urgent" for you?

I was compelled to create, yes, and translate messages.

By MYRINEREST?

That's right.

And she dictates what you should draw or paint?

It's an automatic process that guides my hand. Often she signs her own work.

Do you have *any* control of the outcome?

My hand is completely possessed by her when she enters my body. My art making is a kind of spontaneous graphic activity, prompted by internal and largely unconscious forces.

How often and how long do you work?

Usually I work through the night, every night. Some nights I've produced hundreds of drawings; sometimes I work only on one large piece. My largest is 30 feet long, I'm told.

You used calico fabric, one of my favorites!

The one I think you mean is called "Revelation."

Do you also work during the day?

My day-to-day personality is not flooded by the emergence of unconscious imagery. It is only when I'm possessed by M. that my conscious mind is obscured; otherwise I go about my business as others do.

If I were to let myself go, would a spirit guide me, too?

It's possible. You must listen for it. Be open.

Can you explain what you mean?

I often find myself in a separate reality. When I'm there, I listen. It's not long before something enters my mind obliquely. I "see" out of the corner of my eye. I have an impulse to draw or paint or play the piano. Then I simply begin.

Have you read Carlos Castaneda, by chance?

Who?

Uh, never mind…May I ask, who are the women in your drawings? What do they represent?

I'm not sure. I've never identified them as anyone in particular.

They seem rather fashionable.

MYRNINEREST is very interested in fashion.

The women are often dressed in wonderful hats!

M loves hats, luxurious coats and sometimes feathers.

Your women also have charming features: large eyes and small mouths. How did you come up with them?

I'm glad you like them, but I can't take credit for their appearance; I only share images and messages I receive from the other side.

These women seem trapped in maze-like spaces. How do you explain the frenetic, complex, imagery?

As a medium possessed by spirits I'm expected to move beyond the confines of my limited personality and experience into unfamiliar, frightening territory.

Some are indeed a bit frightening. Yet you have no idea what the images you are compelled to draw represent?

Honestly, I never questioned their meaning.

Is it true you didn't begin working seriously until age thirty-six?

Yes, but I was a wife and mother as well.

Do you find being an artist and a mother challenging?

I suppose so, sometimes. I had three children. Well, four.

And you lost three?

My second son died of the Spanish flu in 1918.

And not even a year later you had a stillborn daughter, and lost your left eye!

The loss was a result of my illness, yes. That made it difficult to see at night, I daresay.

You continued to work, nevertheless.

I suppose I did, with spirit guidance.

You were very prolific, even with one eye! You produced not only drawings and paintings, but an effusion of writing, embroidery, and knitting as well. And played the

piano, I'm told?

Correct. I used to frighten my sons with my glass eye, too.

Your drawings were done on both paper and fabric. Did you ever exhibit your work?

Only a few times in small galleries. The East End exhibition for amateur artists was one.

You received critical acclaim, especially for your work on calico. Did you ever sell any?

No, I dislike publicity, and the work's not mine to sell.

You're very modest. What was your childhood like?

I was sent to an orphanage by my mother when I was nine; then I went to Canada and worked as a servant on a farm until I was nineteen.

Why were you sent to an orphanage?

I was an illegitimate child, and it was 1891.

At nineteen you returned to England to live with your aunt?

Yes, I took a nursing job then.

When was it that she introduced you to spiritualism?

Around 1901.

Eventually you married?

Yes. I was 23 when I married my cousin Tom.

A stockbroker, right?

Yes.

How was the marriage?

The usual, I suppose. After our daughter's death and I became ill, he consorted with other women.

When did you become most active in spiritualist practice?

Not until after Tom died.

That was 1933, the beginning of the war. Did it influence your work to some extent?

The war, or my husband's death?

Both.

Maybe. I did quite a few drawings during and after the war.

I would imagine both events caused a great deal of anxiety.

My second son's death was the most difficult. He died in 1918.

You took to drinking heavily.

Don't we all?

What happened to all the work you produced? Weren't there thousands of drawings left behind?

I hid it all underneath my mattress.

What for?

For MYRNINEREST. It belonged to her.

BALTHUS

*"Painting is a language which cannot be replaced by another language.
I don't know what to say about what I paint, really."*
– Balthus

You prefer to be known as an enigma, notoriously reclusive. Where do I begin?

The best way to begin is to say: "Balthus is a painter of whom nothing is known. And now let us have a look at his paintings."

I know a few things about you, aside from your paintings.

Such as?

You were born in Paris in 1908. Your name was Balthasar Klossowski.

Count de Rola, you might add.

I was going to say that. But the "petty nobility" lineage thing is largely undocumented, right?

Believe what you like. We fly our "Rola" coat of arms proudly.

Where did the name Balthus originate?

A childhood nickname. We spelled it "Balthusz."

You're Polish?

Right.

What part of Poland?

The Prussian part, when such a region existed.

Your son Fumio from your second marriage died of Tay-sachs disease. Would that mean your heritage is also Jewish?

Where did you hear that?

Your biographer told me.

That hasn't really been confirmed.

You were raised in Paris, Geneva, and Berlin?

Right. And later in life I lived in Rome and then returned to Switzerland.

What else?

I love cats.

You dubbed yourself the King of Cats!

And adolescent girls.

I'll get to that later, but first: cats. Tell me about Mitsou.

The book, or the cat?

Both, please.

Mitsou was a cat I had when I was eleven. He ran away,

and I became depressed. I made forty drawings that were eventually compiled into a book that told the story of how I loved and lost him.

Mitsou was published in 1921. You were thirteen?

Yes. The poet Rainer Maria Rilke wrote the introduction.

Rilke was your mother's lover?

Where did you hear that?

It's been well-documented.

Rilke was a good friend of the family. Mother was a painter [named Baladine Spiro]. Father was a painter and an art historian. Our family friends were all rather distinguished within the arts.

Didn't you have an older brother who was a writer?

[Balthus yawns.] Pierre was a philosopher and writer influenced by theology and the works of the Marquis de Sade.

You must have been a precocious child. How did you learn to paint?

I was mostly self-taught. I copied the old masters in the Louvre in the beginning, but didn't undergo any formal training.

Your influences were mainly Renaissance?

Oh, I was influenced by Piero della Francesca and Poussin, but there was also Courbet, Cézanne, de Chirico, Ingres, Goya, and even Lewis Carroll and Emily Brontë, among others.

When was your first exhibit?

In Paris in 1934. I was twenty six.

Is it true you scandalized the audience there with your painting "The Guitar Lesson"?

I should never have painted that one. I got no end of criticism and grief about it.

What did you expect in 1934? A young female teacher with a child over her knee, the child's genitals exposed, the teacher strumming her like a guitar?

I'm not sure what you're suggesting. There is nothing erotic about the models in my paintings, in any case. I think of all my angels as having a kind of sacred quality.

I admit, your paintings are sublime. Wouldn't you agree they depict figures in enigmatic narrative compositions, especially semi-aware pubescent girls placed in situations of riveting mystery, ambiguous eroticism, and a light that transfixes time?

[Balthus shrugs.]

Is it true you had affairs with your adolescent models, including George Bataille's daughter [Lacan's step-daughter] Laurence Bataille?

I don't remember. But I made a nice series of paintings of her visits. One is called "The Week of Four Thursdays." [1949]

That's the painting in which teen age Laurence reclines in a loose robe, playing with a cat?

Yes, she grew up to be a psychoanalyst like her father, Jacques Lacan. Nice girl…

And your neighbor's eleven year old daughter, Thérèse Blanchard, pictured in several of your paintings from 1936?

I made ten paintings of her between 1936 and 1939. Some say they were my finest paintings.

They certainly have a surreal quality. Are you sure you didn't have an affair with her?

An affair? I don't recall. She was one of my most inspiring muses, I do remember that.

Antoinette de Watteville was also a subject. She agreed to marry you in 1937 after having refused your initial proposal several years prior.

She was a good model; from a socially prominent Swiss family. I wooed her for four years, but she was already engaged to a diplomat. Eventually she broke off with him, we were married, and had two sons.

Didn't her initial refusal cause you to attempt suicide with laudanum?

I was upset, yes. Thank goodness my friend Artaud found me in time!

Your painting of Antoinette in "Girl in Green and Red" [1944] marks one of your closest approaches to Surrealism. How is it that you didn't consider yourself as part of the Surrealists?

My first exhibit in 1934 at Gallerie Pierre in Paris was associated with the Surrealists. I was intrigued by the sexual implications of dreams that they initially explored, but I was never seduced by their love of the irrational, I suppose.

It's easy to see why the Surrealists wanted to adopt you, don't you agree?

Sure. They wanted to claim me as one of their own for displaying a sense of the anti-bourgeois, liberated libido.

Is that what you intend your paintings to convey? What is your approach to painting?

Painting what I experience, translating what I feel is like a great liberation. But it is also work, self-examination, consciousness, criticism, struggle.

Haven't you also said that you try to paint as if you are the mediator between you and the universe?

I would often pray for that, yes. To let go of my ego so that I could become the vessel through which the spirit of the universe could paint.

I've read you considered yourself one of the last real painters, is that accurate?

Painting for me was a precise ritual, like a prayer. I worked in my studio religiously from 9 – 5 daily, even having lunch there, only going home for tea time.

Your daughter Haruki said that painting seemed to be religion for you.

I had strict working habits, you might say.

She also said you had very strong opinions about contemporary art and artists. You told her, for example that you

were the last real painter. What did you mean by that?

Artists in current times are limited. One should always know what's been done before and have respect for the masters. A painter should know how to make his own colors, for example. I believe artists should master the old traditions before trying new things.

Ultimately, did you find your own work to be satisfactory?

Painting is a source of endless pleasure, but also of great anguish.

What do you mean? Is self-expression so problematic?

For me, painting is the passage from the chaos of the emotions to the order of the possible. I find the process difficult, but also extremely rewarding.

The atmosphere of your lavishly brushed paintings from the thirties onward seem all the more charged for being contained within an architectonic structure as classically calm and balanced as those of Piero della Francesca and Nicolas Poussin. Was that intentional?

I tried to let the paintings happen intuitively.

The result is an eerie sense of the anxiety and decadence that haunted postwar Europe.

It *was* a time of anxiety. Perhaps the paintings convey a subconscious sense of imbalance that permeated all life.

Some say they experience a sense of attraction-repulsion when confronted with your work. How do you respond?

What do you mean?

Your painting draws the viewer in and there is a sense of voyeurism that is both attractive and repulsive, you must admit, given the nature of the subject matter.

Again you speak about the subject matter. I painted other subjects other than girls and cats. Landscapes and cityscapes, for example. And I produced sets for the theatre.

It's true, eroticism fades in your later work: there's a flatness conveyed through simplified figures and rather dull, tortuously worked surfaces of matte

pigment. Your original Renaissance-like frescoes remain evocative, nevertheless.

I suppose my pretentiousness survived my passion.

Speaking of passion, your second wife was 36 years younger?

Setsuko. Also an artist. We had many happy years together.

[As if by rote, the lovely Setsuko appears, carrying a black lacquer tray with a steaming pot of Japanese Cherry Sakura tea and teacups.]

You lived to be ninety-two. How is it that you were able to remain so enigmatic for so many years?

[Balthus motions to a painting on the wall, "The Guitar Lesson," as Setusko pours tea.]

I always felt the desire to look for the extraordinary in ordinary things; to suggest, not to impose, to leave always a slight touch or mystery in my paintings. I think I succeeded.

BÉLA LUGOSI

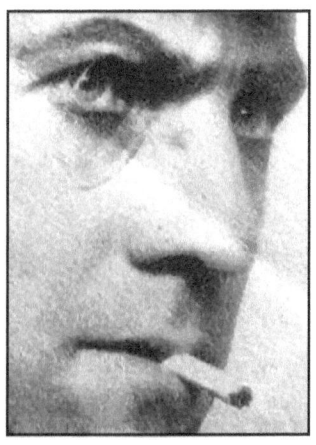

"I have never met a vampire personally, but I don't know vhat might happen tomorrow."
– Béla Lugosi

I'm sitting in a 1920s-style ballroom having a drink at the Savoy Hotel in Budapest, near the river. Tug boats chug by, occasionally sounding their horns, orchestra music is playing. The windows are open, allowing a cool breeze to drift in. I'm elegantly dressed, waiting for Lugosi to arrive. He finally appears half an hour late, eyes glowing. 6 foot 1, about 180 pounds, he's wearing a white shirt with a stiff, starched collar and a black jacket, bowtie, and a short black cape. I stand, shake his hand and motion for him to sit down.

Forgive me to be so late, I vas detained.

Good of you to agree to do the interview, Béla.

Normally I do not do such things. This is my pleasure, however. Vee are kindred souls, in a vay.

How so?

Birthdays. They are two days apart, yours and mine.

That's true. October 18th and 20th.

Children of the night!

I, uh... yes...

Vee both have Eastern European roots, as vell!

True, my background is Croatian-Romanian.

Croatia vas part of Austro-Hungarian Empire. I am from Hungary, from Transylvanian region!

I know.

Your surname has qvite a history!

What do you mean? On my father's side?

A Romanian name, yes?

Yes. My paternal grandfather's name was Matei Ivanovici.

But he changed it to Ivan Matthews during McCarthy era?

That's right. My father was born Matthews; he returned to his father's name Ivanovici later in life.

Dat's vat I thot.

And you? Is Béla Lugosi your real name? Where were you born?

I vas born Béla Ferenc Dezcő Blascó, in Lugos, Hungary.

You took the name Lugosi after your hometown Lugos?

Correct. In Transylvanian region.

[I feel a chill, as if an icy wind has blown the curtains on the open windows.]

Won't you have a drink? I'm having white wine.

I don't drink vine [he chuckles softly]. Perhaps just one glass. Red.

When did you leave Hungary, and how did you find your way to the U.S.?

I first entered country at New Orleans in December, 1920.

You were already twenty-eight. Didn't I hear you had an acting career in Hungary before you emigrated?

I did [sipping his drink].

Care to elaborate?

I vas leading actor of Hungary's Royal National Theatre!

Weren't those mostly small, supporting roles?

[He winces] I do not remember.

In any case, you were self-taught? Didn't you drop out of school?

Yes, I ran avay to be vith my sister and join acting company.

I read you were an activist in the Hungarian Revolution.

I helped vorm Hungarian actors' union, 1913.

But first you enlisted as an infantryman during World War I?

Yes. I rose to rank of captain in ski patrol and vas avarded medal for vounds I suffered vhile serving on Russian front.

Impressive!

I vas also performing Shakespeare, by da vay.

[I order another drink.]

But due to your activism during the revolution of 1919 you were forced to flee your homeland.

Yes, is true. I vent first to Vienna and then settled in exile in Berlin in the Langestrasse.

You continued acting in Berlin?

I made tvelve silent vilms in Hungary between 1917 and 1918, using stage name Arisztid Olt, before leaving for Germany.

You made films in Germany, as well?

Of course.

Were they well-received?

I vas famous actor in Europe.

So, you made your way to New York. When was that?

1921. I verked as laborer for some time—I vas big man! I later entered theater in New York City's Hungarian immigrant colony.

And formed a small stock company that toured Eastern cities, playing for immigrant audiences, is that right?

My first Broadvay play, *Red Poppy*, vas in 1922. First American (silent) vilm role vas in 1923, *The Silent Command*.

What other roles did you play?

I had several more silent vilm roles, mostly as villains, continental types, dat kept me busy in New York.

You were first approached to appear in *Dracula* as a Broadway play, right?

It vas adaptation of Bram Stoker's novel.

And eventually you were called to Hollywood for early talkies.

Do you know? Hollyvood not choose me at first for vilm role of Dracula.

[Béla's eyes seemed to simultaneously darken and grow bigger. A shiver ran down my spine, yet for reasons I cannot explain, I felt a strange attraction to him.]

The rumor was that Lon Chaney was Universal's first choice for the role, and that you were chosen only due to his death shortly before production.

Dat is quvestionable, because Chaney's long-term contract vith Metro, negotiated just bevore his death vould have prevented it, you see.

Really?

Oh yes [raises his hand and snaps fingers for the waitress].

—*Another glass of wine, sir?*—

No! Bring me Pálinka!

[the waitress nods and bows away]

Your performance as Count Dracula on the American stage garnered you much attention as it was unlike any previous portrayals of the role, and after a six month run on Broadvay—excuse me, on Broadway—you toured the United States to much fanfare and critical acclaim throughout 1928 and 1929.

Indeed, Broadvay play vas so successful that Universal decided to make movie vith me as star! Da rest is heestoree, as dey say.

Is there any truth to the rumors of your rivalry with Boris Karloff, or was it concocted by studio publicists?

Karloff vas alvays getting top billing at Universal. He tried upstage me!

Is it true that because of his success you were typecast and couldn't break out of monster roles?

I tried to convince Universal to give me leading roles in other vilms, but Karloff vas deir man.

Universal eventually changed management in 1936 and there was a British ban on horror films, right?

I vas annoyed at afternoon tea habit of Karloff's, mostly.

Horror films went out of fashion around that time, didn't they?

[Bela's eyes seemed to glow white hot, emanating an eerie light —I couldn't look away.]

I vas consigned to Universal's non-horror B-vilm unit, performing small parts vhere I vas used for my name only. Imagine!

Perhaps your accent limited your roles, as well?

Vat do you mean?

[I'm not sure if the wine is getting to me, or it's something about Béla's stare, but I'm feeling slightly light-headed. I pressed on...]

Since Boris Karloff was preferred by Universal, you accepted leading roles from independent producers – low-budget thrillers that helped you financially not artistically, isn't that right?

I vas happy to be in vilms of Ed Vood!

I believe *Plan 9 From Outer Space* was your last film. It's been called the worst movie ever made.

I did not live to vinish the vilm, so I did not vorry about it. I believe dey used Eddy Vood's vife's chiropractor as my double. He vas physically looking a little bit different from me, but vit da final edits, he made it verk.

[Bela motions to the waitress and orders another round.]

Can we talk about your addiction and rehab?

Because of my injury, you mean?

Your back injury from World War I caused your addiction to morphine?

Of course!

How did it start?

Morphine? I tink maybe vhen tings veren't going so vell vit

films, it began getting vorse. I had addiction long time.

But surely you took the drugs for your severe sciatica pain?

[Beyond the din of the crowded dining room the maitre'd calls out "Van Helsing, party of two!"]

Doktor gave prescription drugs. Vee tried home remedies, but nothing verked.

Morphine, Demerol, alcohol, domestic problems? What about those?

I don't remember everytink. I vas married vive times, you know? Perhaps I vas no good at relationships.

[I catch the sideways glance of an elderly gentleman, being seated along with his dining companion at the next table, and suddenly feel a surge of energy.]

Your fifth wife was 30+ years younger. Didn't she begin writing you letters when you were in rehab?

Vee vere married vhen I got out, right avay.

What happened?

She thot she vould marry Count Dracula! I vas different in real life.

How do you mean?

I vas not charming star I had been, you see.

You must have had financial problems, as well?

[Béla shrugs.]

Is it true you asked to be buried in your cape?

That vas my vife and son Béla Jr.'s idea, not mine.

You must admit, the cape was a nice touch?

[Béla slumps in his chair, glances at his watch.]

One final question before you go. Are you actually dead?

[Béla violently raises his cape over his face and hisses. I feel a chill once again and turn in my seat to retrieve my wrap from the back of the chair. At that moment, I feel a strange sensation, dizzy and and exhausted. Suddenly the room goes black.]

When I come to, the room is empty. I quickly gather my evening bag and shoulder wrap and make my way across to the powder room for a glance in the mirror. Two red marks like puncture wounds swell and glow upon my neck. As I rifle through my bag for some makeup, a windy noise like bat wings startles me. I look up, but see only my reflection and an open window behind me.

AGATHA CHRISTIE

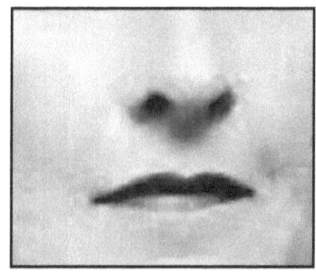

"I have sometimes been wildly, despairingly, acutely miserable, racked with sorrow, but through it all I still know quite certainly that just to be alive is a grand thing."
– Agatha Christie

"Modesty forbade Miss Marple to reply that she was, by now, quite at home with murder." —Agatha Christie, *Murder with Mirrors*

I was to meet Dame Agatha at Cozy's Tea Shoppe at 2 pm. I took the one o'clock from London and descended from the train's second class coach at half past one at St. Mary Mead's main station. It was November and a thick fog blanketed the sky, obscuring plumes of steam that billowed up from the train's sooty tracks, while scurrying passengers' breath evaporated like clouds of smoke into the frozen air.

I pulled my felt cloche over my ears, wrapped my houndstooth scarf snugly round my neck and buttoned the top of my tweed jacket. The blue-capped porter who had retrieved my luggage from the train's underbelly lingered, presumably expecting a tip.

"D'you happen to know the way to Cozy's Tea Shoppe?" I inquired.

"Yes, ma'am, it's only a short distance from here, and close to your hotel. Will you be requiring a taxi?"

"That would be very kind," I admitted, relieved to find at least one of the locals to be just as pleasant as I had read about in some of Christie's mysteries. "I'll need to transport my luggage to the hotel, I'm afraid."

It was a small village, after all, but small villages can often be fraught with secrecy and deception, not to mention unseen malice of various kinds. I was relieved that so far my journey had gotten off to a good start.

"I'll just order the taxi then," he said pleasantly, motioning to his colleague for assistance. I tipped the porter a sixpence, withdrew a cigarette from my cigarette case and had a smoke while I waited.

The taxi soon arrived, whisking me off to Flora G's B & B. After depositing my suitcase and freshening up I made my way on foot to Cozy's Tea Shoppe, near the centre of town. Passing the vicarage, I noticed the roses in the garden had been cut back, in preparation for winter. *Those roses must be lovely in spring*, I mused, continuing on briskly, enjoying the crisp air. *Ugly old thorn bushes now.*

As I walked church bells began to chime. I noticed in passing that the heavy curtain on the vicarage's top floor window was slightly askew and a figure seemed to be watching, though I couldn't be sure. Concentrating on my destination I soon found my way past the church steeple, down a verdant country lane and into the town's cobble-stoned main square, where the various local merchant shoppes were neatly lined up in a row. Cozy's Tea Shoppe was the last on the second block, near the fountain. The windows had lace curtains and a warm glow emanated from within. I opened the glass-paned door, and a cheery bell tinkled as I stepped inside.

Dame Agatha sat in a corner in the very back of the large room scattered with lace-covered tables and elderly ladies having tea. She had short, curled, grey hair and wore thick, black-rimmed glasses and pearls. I extended my hand and she took it weakly, motioning for me to sit down.

"Good of you to come all this way," she said.

"Not at all," I countered. "I've been wanting to meet you for ages. I've been a fan my entire life."

"That's very kind. Well, fire away, then. I won't have much

time, I'm afraid. Will you have tea? I haven't ordered."

"I'd love some," I nodded.

A frilly-aproned waitress arrived and I ordered a pot of Earl Grey tea and a plate of home-made blueberry scones, Cozy's specialty. Dame Agatha had the same. I noticed the waitress wore a gold necklace with a small blue-green charm that dangled as she wiped our table. It appeared to be an Egyptian ankh. I intended to ask about it, but Dame Agatha was waiting.

"May I begin with your biography? When and where were you born?"

"I was born Agatha May Clarissa Miller on September 15th, 1890 in Torquay in Devon, England. Near the seaside, you know."

"Forgive me, but is it true you came from a wealthy, middle-class family?"

"At first we were wealthy, however financial troubles surfaced after my father's death."

"Wasn't your father American? What happened to him?"

She looked at me for a long moment, half-smiled and said, "My mother's second husband was American; he died of heart failure. I'm not sure about my real father."

"That must have been difficult for your mother," I offered.

"Yes, she became quite ill and we decided to travel to cheerier climes. Cairo, for example, and France. We made several trips to Egypt when I was a girl. Eventually I attended finishing school in France in 1905."

"What did you do in Cairo?"

"We went for a three month 'season,' both for my mother's health, of course, and for my coming out. I attended society balls and such, to meet other young people. I didn't know it at the time, but I was to become infinitely enamored with Egypt and the Middle East."

"You're referring to your marriage later in life to Sir Max Mallowan, the archeologist?"

Agatha nodded. "My second husband's profession was a tremendous influence, of course."

"He was fourteen years younger, as I understand. How long were you married?"

"From 1930 to 1976. He survived me, of course."

"How did you meet?"

"We met during an archeological dig, you see. I had always wanted to take a train trip on the Orient Express and a year or so after my split with Archie, I did just that."

"You mentioned a dig?"

"A friend convinced me to visit Ur, an archeological dig in Egypt that my friends the Woolleys ran. During my second visit, Max and I met and found we were excellent companions to each other. Ah, here's our tea."

The waitress had returned with two individual pots and delicate teacups and set everything on the table in front of us. I was going to ask her about the ankh, but she had already concealed it beneath her blouse.

"Those travels," continued Agatha when the waitress was out of earshot, "contributed to my interest in mysticism and middle-eastern mythology."

"And your first husband? How long were you married to him?"

"Archibald Christie and I were married from 1914 to 1928."

"Any children?"

"We had a daughter, Rosalind Hicks."

"Did you enjoy being a grandmother to Rosalind's daughter?"

"Immensely. I was a bit like Miss Marple in the end, I daresay."

"Wasn't Marple your favorite character?"

"Admittedly I was fonder of her than I was of that egoist, Hercule Poirot. Miss Marple was based on my grandmother."

"When did you begin writing stories? Were you always creative?"

Agatha made a dismissive gesture. "At 18, I'd say I was a bit more bored than creative. It was all for fun. Kept me out of trouble, I should think." She smiled and took a sip of tea. "I also took piano and singing lessons, but it was on a dare from my sister actually that I really began writing and then publishing stories."

"You had an unusual upbringing in that you were home-schooled by your father. Your mother was a storyteller and was said to be a psychic with the gift of seeing. How did this contribute to your own story-telling?"

"It all had great influence, I'm sure."

"Are you aware that you hold the record for being the best-selling novelist of all time, and that your novels have sold roughly two billion copies?"

"Why, I suppose not. That's so nice to hear."

"Your estate claims your works come third in the rankings of the world's most widely published books, only behind Shakespeare's works and the Bible?"

"Well, I'll be jiggered!" she exclaimed.

"Then you probably don't know that the best-selling mystery ever—one of the best-selling books of all time—is *And Then There Were None*. Over 100 million in sales to date!"

"Oh my, that's quite a lot. I had no idea, really. It took me quite a long time to find a publisher in the beginning. In the end, of course, I chose the publishers I wanted."

The waitress returned with a plate of warm scones served with strawberry jam and clotted cream, and set them in the middle of the table. Agatha eagerly put the fattest one on her plate and began slathering it with jam and cream.

"When did you become Dame Agatha Christie?"

"1971, I think. Queen Elizabeth II kindly bestowed that honour upon me at Buckingham Palace for my contribution to English Literature."

"And when was it, again that you met Archie, your first husband?"

"It was during one of my débutante seasons – 1912 – he was an aviator in the Royal Flying corps. We were married on Christmas Eve, 1914." She frowned slightly, as if the tea didn't agree with her, then patted her lips with a napkin." We were separated immediately as he was sent to France to fight the Germans…"

"The separation must have caused a strain on your relationship?"

"Oh, it did, but I kept quite very busy as a dispensary nurse."

"Did you go abroad as well?"

"No, I joined the V.A.D. in 1914 to help wounded soldiers in Torquay while Archie was in France."

"Dispensary work must have been taxing for a creative young woman such as yourself. How did you manage to survive the drudgery?"

She slid her cup off to the side and looked at me evenly.

"I became certified in poisons."

I bit my lip to keep from smiling.

"I had no idea!" I said.

The waitress came by to see if we needed anything. As she cleared one of the extra plates I could have sworn I saw something drop from her sleeve, but she quickly cleared up and moved along to the next table.

"I received my certification," said Agatha, matter-of-factly. "After passing my exam, of course, at the Society of Apothecaries. Do have another scone."

"Were you given any kind of recognition for this accomplishment?"

"Well, I did receive a nice review in the *Pharmaceutical Journal,* which was probably unprecedented for a fiction writer."

"What happened when Archie returned home from France?"

"He was offered the job of helping organise a world tour to promote the British Empire Exhibition, which was to be held in London in 1924. We travelled across what was then the British empire—South Africa, Australia, New Zealand, Hawaii. We were among the first Britons to surf standing up!"

"I don't believe it! I didn't know you surfed!"

"Oh yes indeed, I was quite good at it, you see. The surf boards in South Africa were made of light, thin wood, easy to carry, and one soon got the knack of coming in on the waves. It was occasionally painful as you took a nosedive down into the sand, but on the whole it was an easy sport and great fun."

"What kind of surfing gear did you wear??"

"To protect our feet, we bought soft leather boots. I swapped my silky bathing outfit for something a little more practical but equally stylish: A wonderful, skimpy emerald green wool bathing dress, which was the joy of my life, and in which I thought I looked remarkably well!"

"Bravo!"

"I was quite a sporting young woman, with quite a passion for the sea, I must say!"

"You were also quite successful with your writing by then."

"Yes, I had published several books, including *The Mysterious Affair at Styles* and several Poirot short stories. I divided my time between my daughter and my writing. Archie had his golf."

"Is that how he met Nancy Neale?" I asked.

"Through golf? Yes, I suppose."

"Forgive me for asking, but was Archie's affair the cause of your disappearance?

Agatha leaned back slightly and seemed to weigh her response.

"My mother had recently died. I knew Archie had a mistress and we quarreled. He wanted to spend the weekend with Nancy in Surrey."

"Is that what led to your disappearance? You've never spoken about it to anyone."

"It was early one night in December... they say I left Rosalind with the maids without saying where I was going."

"Your car," I said, "a Morris Cowley, was found abandoned the next morning several miles away at Newlands Corner perched above a chalk quarry with an expired license and all your clothes! It was in all the papers!"

"Don't believe everything you read in those horrid newspapers. In point of fact, I *left* a letter for my secretary saying I was going to Yorkshire."

"You disappeared for 11 days! There was a nationwide search! Where did you go?"

"I checked in at the Swans Hydropathic hotel in Harrogate, under the name Theresa Neale of South Africa."

That struck me as right out of one of her novels. Even the name, Theresa Neale, her husband's mistress's name, of all things!, was pure A.G. She could probably see the excitement in my eyes.

"How did they find you?"

"I was recognized by hotel staff who alerted the police. And they called for Archie. But when he arrived to pick me up I didn't recognize him. I honestly couldn't remember where I was or who I was. It all seemed like a dream."

She raised a hand to her brow, briefly closed her eyes.

"May I ask just a few more questions?"

She shook her head. "This, I'm afraid. is the end, she said, weakly, suddenly looking pale. "I've been poisoned, you see. I knew it at least an hour ago when the waitress brought our tea. A poisoned capsule fell out of her sleeve and into my tea. The minute I saw the ankh charm dangling from her necklace I knew she was the same woman I'd met on an archeological dig at Ur many years ago. She'd always loved Max, but her love was unreciprocated. He toyed with her, of course, before I came along, but with me it was true love. She could never forgive either of us for that. In the end I die twice, I'm afraid. Once in 1976 and once again now, here, in St. Mary Meade, Miss Marple's home. It's just as well, as Jane was always my favorite character. I must thank you for your excellent questions, my dear, and I wish you all the best with your book. You've managed quite well, I'd say. Forgive me, but I must go lie down now. I have a room upstairs, you see. Goodbye."

With that, Dame Agatha rose unsteadily from her chair as the waitress with the frilly-apron appeared at her side and helped her quietly up the stairs.

ANONYMOUS

"Drawing on my fine command of language, I said nothing."
— Anonymous

Thanks for agreeing to do the interview.

My pleasure.

I'm not sure I know where to begin.

You've said that before.

Have I?

Yes, you've said that with many of your artists in this book.

Have I? I'm saying it again.

Who are you?

Don't you know?

Enlighten me.

I'm the one your mother warned you about.

Don't kid me.

I'm here and there and everywhere.

Now you're really getting cliché.

I would never do that (intentionally).

So what do you want this interview to be about?

We could start with your biography as we've done with so many of the other artists.

But then I wouldn't be Anonymous.

True.

Where were you born?

California.

That must have been a nice place to grow up.

It was.

What else?

I love the ocean.

Were you always creative?

Yes, and no.

What do you hope to achieve with your creative endeavors?

Evoke dreams, memory, negative space, film, visual

imagery, and sound by employing assonance and dissonance, among other things.

I thought you only wrote dialogue?

I like to write different things. Rooted in haiku and conceptual art, my "conceptual writing" does not adhere to one tradition or another, nor does it claim to be completely innovative.

Are you referring to your earlier art and writing blog posts?

Pairing the banal with the dramatic, the fictional with the (sur)real, the sublime and the profane: the combination of text and images attempts to reflect a symbiosis that would cultivate a sensory as well as intellectual experience.

Sounds profound.

I thought it sounded important.

Art and writing is important.

Many don't see it that way.

Yet we continue creating.

How long have you felt that way?

As long as I've been around.

How long is that?

Since the beginning of time.

What have you learned since then?

You were about to say, "if anything," right?

That's right. Well?

Look, this isn't "goodbye" or anything. Just the finale to your book.

I know, I'm just feeling a bit sentimental.

Morose, is more like it.

Sorry.

What have I learned? That there is always more to be learned.

Now you're sounding like a philosopher.

I can be philosophical, now and then.

Nothing wrong with that.

And the spiritual? Have you cultivated a sense of the spiritual in your endeavors?

Oh, definitely.

How so?

Intuition. Trust. Love.

Love!?

How many artists haven't been affected by love in one way or another?

Love is everything.

Nobody understands that.

Well, maybe John Lennon did.

And moonlight. A lot can be said about moonlight.

Like Yoko Ono's moonlit houses?

It's about imagination.

I see that now.

But it takes a good deal of courage to get there.

I agree.

And childishness.

You mean, play.

And how can you hope to summarize everything that has ever happened creatively in the history of time?

I can't. I can only hope to pay homage.

Teaching.

What?

Artists are teachers.

What's that you say?

Artists are teachers. We all teach each other. That's what I've learned.

You can't just make sweeping statements without presenting any evidence to back them up with anything.

Oh, can't I?

I mean, this isn't a kind of Socratic dialogue, is it?

I don't know about Socratic. Dialogue, yes.

What's the point, then?

The point of what?

This conversation.

The point is that we agree.

What should we agree on?

Maybe we won't agree, but at least we should at least reach a consensus.

About what?

A universal truth.

Oh dear. And what truth would that be?

In my experience, there are many universal truths. The meaning of art, for example.

I see. Shall I tell you what I think?

You could give me an example of your own experience. Then we could discuss. But it shouldn't be too emotional, nor should it be a very recent experience.

I'd like to use writing as an example.

Go ahead, then.

I think creativity takes courage.

Now you're sounding cliché again.

It also takes time.

Agreed.

Are we also in agreement that universal truths are grounded in particular experiences?

I'm not sure.

Madness? Suffering? What of those?

Both fall under the category of "misunderstood genius."

Madmen/women are geniuses?

Sometimes.

Oh! We forgot about humor!

Indeed. Humor is necessary for survival. We could say that's a universal truth, no?

Perhaps.

One last question, since Anonymous has been in the news lately.

Oh, you mean the "loosely associated international protest network of activist and hacktivist entities that has launched cyber-attacks on government and popular culture"?

Yes, that's what I meant.

That's not me.

Then let's pretend this conversation never happened.

My lips are sealed.

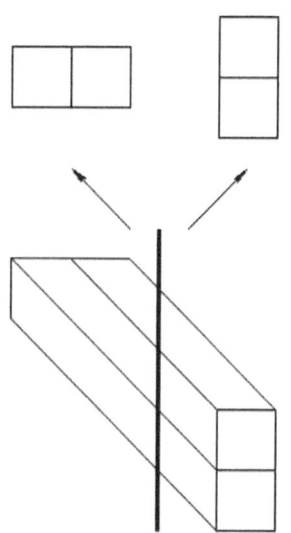

PARTIAL BIBLIOGRAPHY

PUBLISHER'S NOTE: A list of the author's online sources with "live" links is available on our web site at the following URL: **blackscatbooks.com/extras**

And Then There Were None. Agatha Christie. St. Martin's Griffin (1966)

Art Since 1940, Strategies of Being. 2nd Edition. Jonathan Fineberg. Prentice Hall (2000)

Dali, A Study of His Art-in-jewels: The collection of the Own Cheatham Foundation. Owen Cheatham Foundation, New York Graphic Society (1959)

Dialogues with Marcel Duchamp. Pierre Cabanne. Da Capo Press, London (1979)

Forty Images by Balthus. Mitsou Balthus. The Metropolitan Museum of Art. New York (1984)

Grapefruit. Yoko Ono. Simon & Schuster (1964)

The Hearing Trumpet. Leonora Carrington. Exact Change (1996)

History of Modern Art, Painting, Sculpture, Architecture, Photography, fifth edition. H.H. Arneson. Prentice Hall (2003)

Hitchcock. François Truffaut. Secker & Warburg (UK: 1968), Gallimard - *édition définitive* (France: 2003)

Louise Bourgeois. by Robert Storr. Phaidon (2003)

Leonora Carrington, Surrealism, Alchemy and Art. Susan l. Aberth. Lund Humphreys, Ltd. (London: 2010)

The Letters of Vincent Van Gogh. Arnold Pomerans, Translator. Ronald de Leeuw, Editor. Penguin Classics (1997)

Mega Squares. Andy Warhol. Grange Books (UK: 2005)

The Life and Times of Miss Jane Marple. Anne Hart . Dodd, Mead & Co. (1985)

Parallel Visions: Modern Artists and Outsider Art, exhibition catalogue by Maurice Tuchman and Carol S. Eliel (Los Angeles County Museum of Art (1992)

Surrealism. Herbert Read. Praeger (1971)

Fineberg, Jonathan. *Art Since 1940, Strategies of Being.* 2nd Edition. Prentice Hall, New Jersey: 2000

ABOUT THE AUTHOR

Carla M. Wilson has been dabbling in various art forms including drawing, painting, ceramics, music, writing, theater, and film since childhood. She received an MFA in Fiction and has a B.A. in Communications. Her writing and visuals have appeared in *Talking Writing, Fiction International, Black Scat Review, Poetry International, Sleipnir,* and in other online and printed journals. She lives in San Diego, California.

www.ingramcontent.com/pod-product-compliance
Lightning Source LLC
Chambersburg PA
CBHW031407250626
47155CB00004B/1446